Adventures of Biscuit

I Can Read!

Adventures of

Biscuit

Five Stories About
Everyone's Favorite Puppy

by Alyssa Satin Capucilli • pictures by Pat Schories

Sandy Creek

Sandy Creek
387 Park Avenue South
New York, NY 10016

ISBN 978-1-4351-2646-6
Manufactured in China.
Manufactured 06/2011
Lot 11 12 13 SCP 10 9 8 7 6 5 4 3 2

Contents

Biscuit

For Laura and Peter who wait patiently
for a Biscuit of their very own
–A. S. C.

For Tess
–P. S.

This is Biscuit.

Biscuit is small.

Biscuit is yellow.

Time for bed, Biscuit!

12

Woof, woof!

Biscuit wants to play.

Time for bed, Biscuit!

Woof, woof!

Biscuit wants a snack.

Time for bed, Biscuit!

Woof, woof!

Biscuit wants a drink.

Time for bed, Biscuit!

Woof, woof!

Biscuit wants to hear a story.

Time for bed, Biscuit!

Woof, woof!

Biscuit wants his blanket.

Time for bed, Biscuit!

Woof, woof!

Biscuit wants his doll.

Time for bed, Biscuit!

Woof, woof!

Biscuit wants a hug.

Time for bed, Biscuit!

Woof, woof!

Biscuit wants a kiss.

Time for bed, Biscuit!

Woof, woof!

Biscuit wants a light on.

Woof!

Biscuit wants to be tucked in.

Woof!

Biscuit wants one more kiss.

Woof!

Biscuit wants one more hug.

Woof!

Biscuit wants to curl up.

Sleepy puppy.

Good night, Biscuit.

Biscuit, who will you play with today?

Biscuit
Finds a Friend

For two very special friends,
Margaret Jean O'Conner and Willie Hornick.

Woof! Woof!

What has Biscuit found?

Is it a ball?

Woof!

Is it a bone?

Woof!

Quack!

It is a little duck.

The little duck is lost.

Woof! Woof!

We will bring
the little duck
back to the pond.

Woof! Woof!

Here, little duck.

Here is the pond.

Here are your mother
and your father.
Quack!

Here are your brothers
and your sisters.
Quack! Quack!

The ducks say thank you.
Thank you for finding
the little duck.

Quack!
The little duck
wants to play.

Quack!
Woof!

Quack!
Woof!

Splash!

Biscuit fell into the pond!

Silly Biscuit.

You are all wet!

Woof!

Oh no, Biscuit.

Not a big shake!

Woof!

Time to go home, Biscuit.

Quack! Quack!

Say good-bye, Biscuit.

Woof! Woof!

Good-bye, little duck.

Biscuit has found
a new friend.

Silly Biscuit, don't go in the mud!

Bathtime for
Biscuit

This one is for my parents.
–A. S. C.

To Sri K.
–P. S.

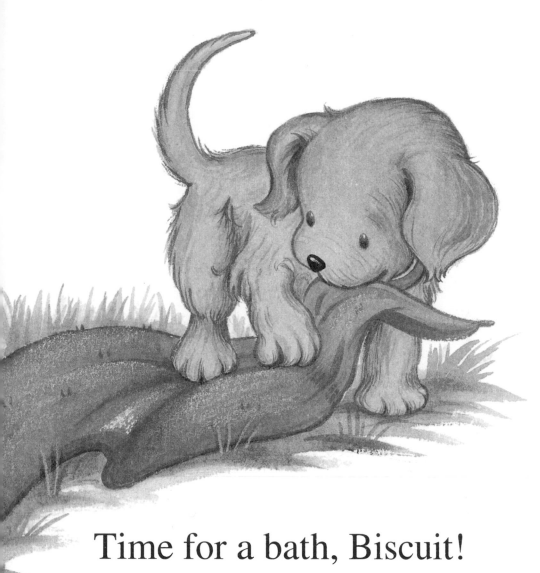

Time for a bath, Biscuit!

Woof, woof!

Biscuit wants to play.

Time for a bath, Biscuit!

Woof, woof!

Biscuit wants to dig.

Time for a bath, Biscuit!

Woof, woof!

Biscuit wants to roll.

Time for a bath, Biscuit!

Time to get nice and clean.

Woof, woof!

In you go!

Woof!

Biscuit does not want a bath!

Bow wow!

Biscuit sees

his friend Puddles.

Woof, woof!

Biscuit wants to climb out.

Come back, Biscuit!

Woof!

Come back, Puddles!

Bow wow!

Biscuit and Puddles
want to play
in the sprinkler.

Biscuit and Puddles
want to dig
in the mud.

Biscuit and Puddles
want to roll
in the flower bed.

Now I have you!

Woof, woof!
Let go of the towel,
Biscuit!

Bow wow!

Let go of the towel,
Puddles!

Silly puppies!

Let go!

Woof, woof!

Bow wow!

Oh!

Time for a bath, Biscuit!

Woof, woof!

A bath for all of us!

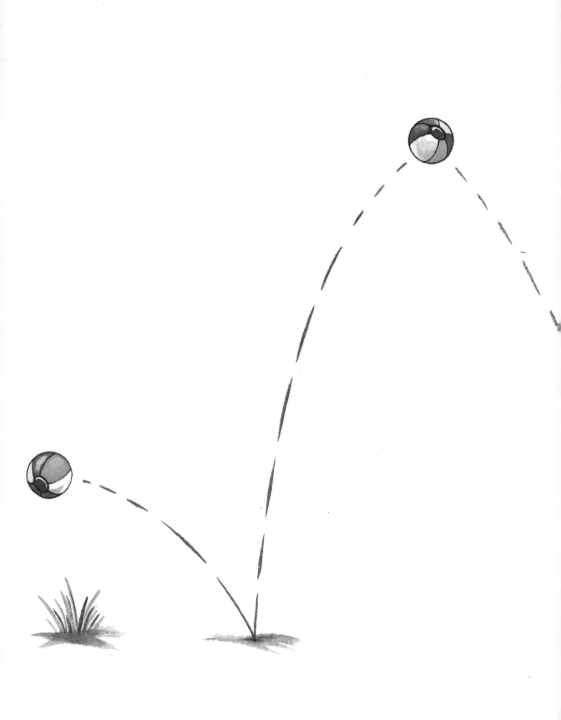

Do you want to learn a trick, Biscuit?

Biscuit's New Trick

For Anthony and Ruby, the newest
—A. S. C.

To Laura
—P. S.

Here, Biscuit!
Look what I have.
Woof, woof!

It's time to learn
a new trick, Biscuit.
Woof, woof!

It's time to learn
to fetch the ball.
Ready?

Fetch the ball, Biscuit.

Woof, woof!

Silly puppy!

Don't roll over now.

Get the ball, Biscuit.

Fetch the ball, Biscuit.

Woof, woof!

Where are you going,
Biscuit?
Woof!

Funny puppy!
Fetch the ball,
not your bone.

Let's try again.

Fetch the ball, Biscuit!

Woof, woof!

Good puppy!
You got the ball.
Woof!

Wait, Biscuit.

104

Bring the ball back!

Woof, woof!

105

Let's try one more time.

Fetch the ball, Biscuit!

Woof, woof!

Oh no!
Not in the mud!

Stop, Biscuit!
Don't fetch it now!
Woof!

Oh, Biscuit!

You did it!

You learned a new trick!

Woof, woof!

Biscuit, what's that noise?

Biscuit
Goes to School

*For the wonderful students, teachers,
librarians, and parents who have
welcomed Biscuit into their schools!*

Here comes the school bus!

Woof, woof!

Stay here, Biscuit.

Dogs don't go to school.

Woof!

Where is Biscuit going?

Is Biscuit going to the pond?

Woof!

Is Biscuit going to the park?
Woof!

Biscuit is going to school!
Woof, woof!

Biscuit wants to play ball.

Woof, woof!

Biscuit wants
to hear a story.
Woof, woof!
Shhh!

Biscuit wants a snack.

Woof, woof!

132

Oh, Biscuit!

What are you doing here?

Dogs don't go to school!

Oh, no!

Here comes the teacher!

Woof!

Biscuit wants
to meet the teacher.
Woof!

Biscuit wants
to meet the class.
Woof, woof!

Biscuit likes school!

Woof, woof!

And everyone at school
likes Biscuit!
Woof!